Lily's Secret
Written by Marion Mike
Illustrated by Laurie Eichhorn
GLAMOROUS
CATERPILLAR

Productions, LLC

Self-esteem programs & products for children
Since 1972

AuthorHouse™
1663 Liberty Drive
Bloomington, IN 47403
www.authorhouse.com
Phone: 1 (800) 839-8640

This book is printed on acid-free paper.

ISBN: 978-1-7283-3297-0 (sc)

Print information available on the last page.

Published by AuthorHouse 10/24/2019

authorHOUSE®

To My Grandchildren

"The Greatest Inside-Secrets"

Accept yourself as you are,
Knowing that your wisdom and courage will sustain you!

Acknowledge your talents,
Knowing they will expand exponentially in directions you never dreamed possible!

Be true to yourself,
Knowing that "Who you are on the inside" is more important than
"What you do" on the outside!

Believe in yourself,
Knowing that "having a failure" isn't "being a failure"!

Share your love and talents with others,
Knowing that the power of "giving" can inspire!

Know how much you are loved,
"Up to the Moon and Beyond" through eternity!

Sitto Marion

In the land of Abalobediah, there lived a caterpillar by the name of Lily. Lily discovered that something very strange was happening to her. All of her friends seemed too busy to pay attention to her any more. Lily felt left out.

Lily was a very shy caterpillar. She watched all the other caterpillars playing and laughing and having a great time. But Lily just stood around, plugged in her ear buds and watched.

“Oh,” thought Lily, “They don't even know I’m alive. What can I do to get their attention? Maybe if I look through some of these fashion magazines that Bella gets, maybe I can get an idea about how to get some attention.”

Bella was a very pretty caterpillar who got everyone's attention. She always looked just right and said just the right thing to make her friends feel good. And she loved fashion!

So Lily borrowed several of her magazines and studied them very carefully.

"Maybe I do need a new look! Maybe then I'll fit in."

Lily spent the entire day cutting out pictures and finding ways to create her new look. She then found all the materials she needed to make the ideas come to life!

"Tomorrow I will be the NEW ME!" Lily shouted with joy. For the first time she was looking forward to joining all of the others on the playground.

Lily woke up earlier than usual to get a head start with designing her new look. Her hip belts, rainbow socks, eyelashes, hat and bling were all ready to go! By the time she got everything on just right, she said, “I’m exhausted!” Just before leaving, she took a selfie, looked at herself in the mirror and gasped,

“Wow! This is the new me!”

Lily was ready
to go! She headed
straight for the park where Jake and his
friends were playing soccer. As she got
closer, she heard Jake gasp, “Who are you?
Are you new here?”

Lily answered quickly, “No! It’s me...Lily. I sit behind you in art class.”

“Oh, Lily...right. Are you wearing one of our art projects?”

“No, Jake. This is the latest ‘in’ look. What do you think?”

Lily could hear the others chuckling behind her. “What’s so funny?” Lily snapped.

"Lily, I think you went a little overboard. We all like you just the way you are. You changed yourself so much that we didn't even recognize you! Instead of adding a little fashion, you disguised yourself and we couldn't even see the real you!"

Lily began to walk away, when Bella stopped her and asked, "Will you come to our Valentine's Day Party? We would all love it if you could!"

"Will I? You bet! I would love to!" It was a mixed up day for Lily. She felt so many different emotions all in one day!

When Lily went home, she began working on her Valentine's Day cards for all her friends. She had a few weeks to get them all done.

Just a few days before the party, something strange began to happen. Jake became a strong and handsome butterfly doing tricks in the air.

Then Bella became a beautiful butterfly with bright golden wings trimmed in blue and orange. These brilliant colors reflected the sun like tiny mirrors that shimmered as she flew gracefully high in the sky.

One by one,
all of Lily's friends got their wings...
but Lily was still just a caterpillar.

"Don't worry Lily, you'll get your wings."
said Bella as she tried to comfort Lily.
But that was not comforting to Lily.
All of her friends were in the air flying
around the ribbon rainbow...Lily was grounded.
Lily tried so hard to keep up with her winged
friends, but her legs just were not fast enough.

Each day Lily checked...no signs of wings sprouting anywhere!

Once again, she felt like she just didn't belong.
She cried herself to sleep that night.

The next day, Lily decided to tell her ladybug friend, Abagail, about this problem. Abagail had an idea. “Lily, why don’t we go to the doctor of caterpillarology and see if she can help?” So together they did just that.

The doctor looked at Lily and after a careful examination, she stated, “Lily there is something wrong. I know you don’t want to hear this, but you will never be a butterfly. You will always be a caterpillar, just like me.”

Lily couldn’t believe what she was hearing. “All the other caterpillars turned into butterflies, why can’t I? It’s not fair!” The doctor continued to talk to Lily for a long time, but Lily was not listening. All she could think about was...

She and Abagail talked on the way home. As Lily said goodbye to Abagail, she pleaded, “Abagail, please do not say anything to the others about this... PROMISE?”

“I promise,” Abagail said reluctantly. “I’ll see you at the party tomorrow!”

“The party tomorrow!” Lily panicked. She thought and thought.

“Just because I will be a caterpillar forever, doesn’t mean they have to know it...at least for now!”

Lily started to gather all the things she needed to make herself a pair of wings. She had a lot of stuff left over from her last project so she just needed a few pieces of elastic, some feathers, and some sparkles. She got the paint, glue, glitter, beads, rubber bands, and threw away those nasty eyelash things.

After hours of work, Lily finally declared, “Done! I did it!

I now have wings! Now, let’s test them!”

She climbed to the top of the table with her brand new set of wings tightly strapped to her back like a backpack.

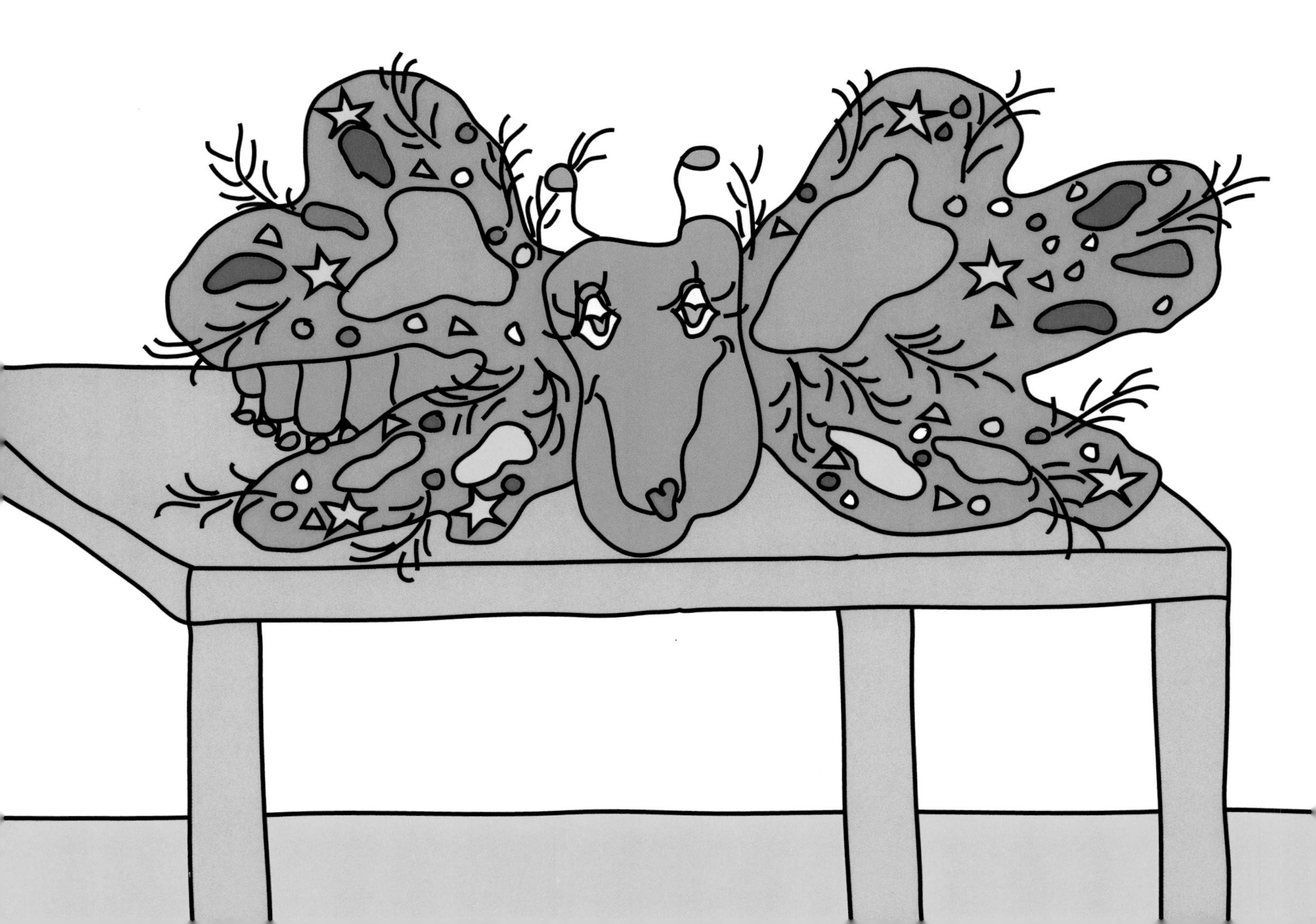

Then she jumped down!
She glided very gently down to the ground for a perfect landing!
"They work! They work!" she screeched with excitement.
Now for the real test... She went to the party.

As soon as Lily arrived, everyone stopped and stared. "Hey look! Lily has her wings! Look how different they are!"

Jake glided down to Lily and said, "I've never seen wings like that before! They're so...so wingy!"

Abagail looked at Lily and couldn't believe her eyes! She wondered, "What is Lily trying to do?"

Jake and Bella yelled to Lily, “Come on, Lily! Join us!
Test your wings. Come fly with us around
the Ribbon Rainbow.”

Lily took a deep breath and started running as fast as she could, flapping her wings faster and faster. She flapped her wings so hard that the elastic belt snapped. The rubber bands broke, and tiny beads and feathers came unglued as the wind blew them through the air.

All of her friends froze in place and gasped, “Oh no! What is happening?” There were feathers and sequins and beads flying through the air, but Lily was still on the ground! She stood in the midst of this mess feeling so embarrassed. There was silence all around. Lily began to cry as she told her friends her secret...she would never be a butterfly... always a caterpillar.

"I just want to fit in and be like all of you. I didn't think you would want to be with me if I couldn't fly."
"Lily, we like you just the way you are. Just be yourself!" said Jake.

“It’s what’s on the inside that counts!”

Bella shouted as she gathered the broken wings and tossed them aside!

"And NO MORE SECRETS!"
I LIKE LILY
JAKE

Other Books in the Series "Once Upon a Time in Abalobediah"

About the Author and Illustrator

Marion Mike is an award-winning public speaker and writer. She is in the Ohio State Hall of Fame for her work in drama. Marion is also a Speech and Language Pathologist living in Corona CA.

Laurie Eichhorn is an award-winning artist and photographer. She is also a freelance graphic designer living in Central Oregon.

I Like Me! Productions, LLC
was created by Marion in 1972 to promote self-esteem in children from pre-school through high school. Marion and Laurie have been working together since meeting in Novato, CA in 1982.

Together they have created many stories, educational materials, seminars and programs for schools and organizations across the nation.

For more information on I like Me! Productions, LLC visit
www.ilikemeproductions.com

Printed in the United States
By Bookmasters